Songs of Dominance

A Songs of Submission Reader

**Jessica
Sharon
Rachel
A Valentine From Jonathan**

by

CD Reiss

The *Songs of Dominance* were released as an experiment. I wanted to write in Jonathan's POV, but did not know how readers would react. So I released *Jessica* to the people on my mailing list. The response was phenomenal, so I released the second story, *Sharon,* to my ever-growing list.

They were traded peer-to-peer on the Goodreads group, CD Canaries, and on my Facebook page. I'd like to thank Canaries Tony, Erik, and Donna for their generosity of spirit in sending out the email repeatedly.

But the stories have become canonical, and things are revealed here that will become important later, so I feel they need to reach a larger audience.

Please read these after *Submit,* or you're going to run into major spoilers. It's best if you read before *Control,* but not a big deal if you read *Control* first.

JESSICA

(This begins after the Eclipse show, when Jonathan drives away from Monica's house)

*****

I watched Monica close the door behind her and felt the car dive off that cliff of a hill. Her house would be a deathtrap in an earthquake, and the hill was probably already falling into the backyard. I considered rectifying it. She was no good to me under forty tons of clay and detritus. She was only any good writhing under my hips like a pinned kitten. God, she was one big nerve ending, that girl, and those big brown eyes got just a little wider when she was close. And those bruises. And how she begged for them.

I knew she was special the night I met her, I just didn't know how special.

I'd gone up to K with Eddie and two other guys from Penn. I was meeting Wendy afterward in one of the hotel rooms. I had one foot in LA from a disaster of a trip to New York, and the other in Seoul for a trip that could not, under any circumstances be anything but a roaring success, or I was going to have to answer questions. I hated answering questions.

So I'd just done the easy thing and took them to K. There had been plenty of nonsense before the tall girl with big, black eyes and long brown hair twisted into braids brought our drinks. The guys were bullshitting about ball and women, when we all stopped to watch waitress come toward us. The night was over. I couldn't take my eyes off her. Everything was in the right place, naturally. My staff has to look as stunning as the guests. But this girl wasn't just beautiful, because they all are, she was something else entirely. I was trying to figure out what it was, and she just looked right back at me, as if daring me to make an even bigger ass of myself.

Then she spilled gin on me, and Freddie fired her. The guys tried to reason with Freddie, but the waitress was gone and I had to let him do his job however he saw fit. I was an hour to Wendy with her legs up in the air and I suddenly found the idea depressing. She was gorgeous and shrill and shallow. She blew too much coke and giggled at all the wrong times. She exhausted me. The thought of another night in one of my hotel rooms drained the life out of my limbs.

Freddie told me the waitress's name, and that she was a sexual harassment case waiting to happen. But I couldn't let the ebony-eyed girl walk away. I had to look at her again. Five minutes. I'd give her a severance. Whatever.

I heard her outside my office and I seized up a little. I wanted to look at her, but had to be discreet. She slipped in, and I wanted to fuck her immediately. She was so long, so curved, so smooth. Her skirt cupped her ass, and her heels brought her to a couple of inches shorter than me. As my eyes dragged over her breasts, and over the length of her neck, I realized she'd seen me looking again. She put her hands on her hips. Definitely a harassment case waiting to happen, especially considering she was telling me about Freddie's fucking stupidity. I looked into her eyes. Fire, and pride. Not an ounce of fear.

What was going on with that gaze was ten times more interesting than the curves of her body.

"I was going to offer you severance," I'd said.

"I don't want your money," she'd shot back.

"Let me finish."

She obeyed not just with her mouth, but her heart. Her face got red and she cast her eyes down. Her fingers twitched, but didn't move otherwise. Holy fuck. I almost lost my breath. This gorgeous, proud creature was submissive.

I couldn't let her walk into Los Angeles and disappear.

And it had only gotten worse since. Of course, I couldn't fall in love with her, even if I tried, but I could pass a lot of time with her. A lot.

I wanted to know every twitch, every growl, every moment of desperate need, and eat her alive. If she needed me to be exclusive, I could do it. I'd just put Sharon on ice and stop looking around. How long could Monica last? A month? Two? How long could she make me laugh before she started asking for more? How many things could leave her lips that would make me want to put my face on hers? She couldn't stay so attractive for long. She'd burn herself out soon enough, but for the time being, I could not have created a more flawless woman.

I felt bad about bruising her, but I hadn't done half the damage her ex-boyfriend's piece had done. What a dick. And as soon as I saw that guy, what he'd done, and the way he looked at her, I wanted her for myself. I knew she was going to ask for exclusivity, I could see it in her face, and once I saw that piece, I was ready to give it to her. The thought of her getting hurt bothered me. It wasn't her personally as much as it was wrong to make their private business so public. It wasn't that hearing her cry made my fist clench, or that I felt as though I saw some shameful part of her she'd wanted to keep hidden. It was an overall, amoral wrongness. Could have been anyone, and I would have been just as mad.

Well, maybe not as mad.

Damn. I should have taken her home. I had a weird compulsion to reach out to her.

—Thank you for tonight. I'll
call you during the week to
check on that baseball—

—You're welcome—

A flat, emotionless response. Odd. I regretted letting her
out of arm's reach.

—Speaking of…They're playing the Mets the day after I
get back—

—Ok good night—

I sat back. Not even a joke or wisecrack. I shouldn't have
cared, but I did. My phone dinged again, but it wasn't Monica
loosening up. It was Jess.

Interesting that Erik wasn't there. He usually followed her
around like a little beta puppy. Exactly what she needed. Half
a man. I took a calming breath and called her.

"Jess."

"Jon. Where are you?"

She didn't sound good, and if I judged the whooshing
background right, she was already home.

"Coming up LFB." Our shortcut for Los Feliz Boulevard,
from when I was whole and had someone to make up little
acronyms with.

"Are you alone?"

"Lil is driving. What's wrong, baby?" I could have guessed
it was Erik, but she'd never admit it.

"Can I see you?"

I looked at my watch. My plane was scheduled out of Santa
Monica at six. I could make it if I left Venice by four. If history was any indication though, I'd be out of there in an hour.

I wished I could tell her no, but we had too much history, too much intimacy to just turn my back. So I let Lil take me home, then I got into the Mercedes and went to Venice.

Again.

***

Jessica lived on the beach, as her publicly sunny demeanor demanded. I parked and walked up the long stairway to the back, where the pool overlooked the ocean. The furniture was gone, as was the barbecue. She stood alone at the half empty bar with her glass of white wine, still wearing her flowing white dress. It outlined the shape of her body in the breeze, making me think immediately of pulling her legs open, but gently. That brought my hot little goddess back to mind, because with her, gentle was optional. I should have nailed her in the car, bruises or no. I wasn't any less aroused than her, and now I was in a dangerous position. I wanted to fuck. I had a weight at the base of my cock that needed to drop, somewhere, somehow.

"Jess," I said when I could see her puffy eyes. "Wasn't there a party or something? After the opening?"

"I couldn't take it any more. Smile, talk about popsicle sticks and culture's effects on childhood memories. Smile. Answer process questions about keeping dead trees alive. Smile again. How are you?"

I snapped a glass off the rack, and Jessica poured me some wine. "I'm fine, really. You called me over here to ask me how I am? It looks like I should be asking you the question."

She barely paused before getting to the point. "Erik."

"I thought you were engaged."

"So did I. Do you want to sit?" She indicated the indoor patio behind sliding glass doors.

The thought of going inside and lounging on a couch with her, which I'd done a hundred times, somehow seemed too risky, so I slid onto a barstool. "Where's everything? Those hideous fucking lamps are gone."

She took a deep breath and swished her wine around. "Three days ago, he took them. They were his."

"Figured." I didn't know what she wanted. Was I supposed to sympathize? She had dozens of girlfriends, each with two shoulders to cry on. What the hell was I doing there?

"He found out you were coming to the opening. And he just went off. 'Why's this guy still hanging around? Why can't you cut him loose?' Blah blah." She downed her wine. "He doesn't understand. Or didn't understand. As you can see, he decided to stop trying, which I guess is for the best."

"I'm sorry to hear it, but I'm not taking the blame for it."

"Jon. You don't have to get defensive."

"Jess. What do you want, if not to blame me?"

She was a bundle of nerves, which no other person would notice because she never wasted a movement. She didn't have a set of sweet little tics like Monica. Jessica was still water, her tension revealed in her gaze, which sat in the middle distance.

"I should be frank," she said.

"You be anyone you want."

"Not funny."

I waited until she was ready, because she'd get to it if I stopped cracking wise, and I had the feeling I would want to hear it.

She took a deep breath. "I think Erik had something. I think he was seeing something I was pretending wasn't there."

She was squirming. Oh, this was good. Delicious even. I didn't say a word. I didn't want to assume she was going where I thought she was because I didn't want the rug pulled from under me again. It wouldn't be the first time she'd implied she wanted me back and then turned the conversation back on itself.

"You've always been there for me." She looked up, right at me.

"We were married," I said. "I told you, I take that seriously."

She took half a step toward me. I'd been through that before with her, and I wouldn't lean into her half a centimeter I didn't have to. I hoped with the same fervor, but I was gun shy. Even when she put her fingers on top of my hand, which she hadn't done in a while, I was torn. After the divorce, she'd still touch me, but she'd back off like a hosed down cat as soon as I went for her. I was impatient with the games and horny as hell from being around Monica. I felt like a caged animal.

So when she touched my face, I froze, convinced I would spin her by the hair and bend her over. That wouldn't do at all. Not if I was going to have her again.

"You're being shy, Jon. That's not like you."

"You going to push me away?"

"No. Not this time."

Fine. I put my hands on the sides of her face so she couldn't turn and pushed her against the bar. I choked off her squeak with a kiss. She kissed me back. She really did.

The drop in my chest was relief. My stomach tightened. To have my life back. To be back to normal again. With my wife at my side, a sealed unit, unbreakable. I touched my old self when I put my hand on her breast. The completed me, at my fingertips.

I pulled her skirt around her hips and hitched her up. She put her legs around my waist, and I carried her inside.

It was dark with those ass-ugly lamps gone. I wanted light to see her, to believe it. Oh, anything could go wrong between us writhing on the couch and me actually getting my dick in her. I remembered my promise to Monica, but I could explain the next day. I'd be sorry to see that sweet thing go, but woman would tolerate infidelity, and I cared too much about both of them to sneak around. Jessica had to be my choice. I'd taken a vow, begged for it to be honored, and waited so long that turning away the possibility of a reunion seemed ludicrous.

I pulled the top of her dress down.

Gorgeous in the moonlight. Those breasts, with little rocks for nipples at the tips. I sucked them and tasted her. The taste of me being normal again. The taste of morning dew and cut grass. I rolled her nipple over my tongue and pushed my hips into her. I whispered her name in a fog of relief and delight. I could barely breathe.

"Are you sure, Jess?" She'd better be sure. Between her and that delicious little girl in Echo Park, I was a throbbing rock.

"Yes, baby. Make love to me like you used to. In the beginning."

Yes, I wanted to. And I might have. If she hadn't asked for the old me back, I might have been as sweet and gentle as our first night. But in my ear, as if she sat right next to me, I heard Monica moan, "Hurt me, Jonathan. Tear me in two." I got even harder, if that was possible, and I was at the point where I could expect to walk out of there with a pair of ten pound weights between my legs. I was too old for that shit.

I faced Jessica. She was beautiful. Exactly the girl I remembered. Her lips were parted, her breathing shallow as she pushed her hips into me. So close. I was so close to having her again.

"I'm sorry, Jess."

"For what?"

"This." I pulled myself off her and sat down by her feet.

She propped herself on her elbows, legs still spread. "What? Why?"

I stroked her calf and looked in her face, half cast in the moonlight. "Because. It's been too much. I just…I can't."

She tucked her legs away and crouched, kneeling by me. She touched my face, and I saw her hurt. She had a deep fear of loneliness. Leaving her alone would undoubtedly be the hardest thing I ever did. "I don't understand," she said. "Is this spite? Or revenge?"

I got up. I owed her honesty, at least, after everything we'd been through, after all I'd promised her, after all the times we'd hurt each other. "It's too late. I'm sorry. I'm not the same man."

"Is it that girl?"

"Which girl?" I knew exactly who she meant. I was suddenly sorry I'd brought Monica to the show. Had I known Erik had walked out, I would have kept her home and writhed around with her all night, just to shield her from my ex-wife's eyes. The thought of that bruised ass, and her attitude about it, even the guilt I'd felt at giving it to her, made my dick twitch to the point of pain. "It's a dalliance, Jess. Don't try to read more into it."

Jessica didn't answer. She just stared at me as if she was reading a book. She must have seen right through me.

"Just go, then," she said quietly.

I wanted to say more, to apologize again or offer some comfort, but in a quarter of a second, I thought better of it. The front door. I just had to make it to the front door. I took long strides, looping my fingers in my keyring as I stepped into the night air. My Mercedes was five steps away. It had been her favorite. That's why I'd brought it. Maybe it was time to get rid of it.

"Jon," she called out. I took another step, getting my hand on the car, not looking back. I didn't want to change my mind. I didn't want another argument. I thought maybe I could get back to Echo Park in time to not make a rude ass of myself in front of Monica.

I couldn't pretend I hadn't heard Jessica. I looked back, just to say good-bye. I didn't see her immediately, but once my eyes scanned the front walk, I saw her, balled up on the ground.

The visit was getting more dramatic than I'd anticipated. Did she feel this way when I'd gotten on my knees and begged her to stay? I'd been such a mess of tears I couldn't remember her expression. God, I'd never do that again.

She cradled her arm. I went to her, and from the way she looked at me, I knew I wasn't getting to my little goddess of Echo Park that night.

***

Dr. Fuhr was in Aruba, but a few phone calls and he'd managed to get us skipped ahead in the emergency room if we could get to Cedars in twenty minutes. It was late enough that the 10 was clear, and we zipped along with the top up, an ice pack on Jessica's arm and a sulk on her face.

"She's pretty," Jessica said.

"Who?" I asked as if I didn't know.

"The girl from tonight. Are they all that pretty?"

"Mostly," I lied.

She looked out the window. "Do they all let you fuck them the way you like it?"

The foul language brought my breath in. That wasn't her way of speaking, and her tone prodded. I took the bait because it was late, my balls ached, and Dr. Fuhr hadn't been available.

"How do I like it, Jess? Maybe you can just repeat back to me what you told all your friends?"

"I needed to tell someone!"

"Everyone. You told everyone that I wanted to beat you. Beat you?"

"You changed, Jon. I was scared."

We'd been through it so many times, the tracks of the argument were smooth and well worn, but that felt different. It felt like the last time.

"I changed because you changed me. And I'll always be grateful. You made me right with myself."

"And right with yourself means you want to tie women up and hurt them."

"I don't want to hurt anyone. You're so fucking vanilla, Jess. It's like a religion. You can't see outside it."

I turned into the ER at Cedars, not facing her until I parked. Tears dampened her face. I hadn't heard her crying in the white noise of the freeway.

I put my hand on hers, but she shook it off.

"I wish we could go back to the way we were," she said.

"I don't."

***

Erik came an hour later, as she was in the x-ray room. We shook hands like gentlemen.

"Nothing happened," I told him. "She's all yours."

The blonde lock drooping over his forehead swayed. He owned a surfboard company, but his face was permanently tanned from twenty years on the waves. "She never was."

"Well, honestly, this is the last time I'm coming running. I'm done. And I'm sorry I had my foot in your yard for so long."

We shook hands again, and I put my hand on his arm because I was really, terribly sorry I'd caused him grief over a woman who was completely wrong for me.

***

It wasn't until I got on the 10 that I started to feel as if a weight had been lifted from my shoulders. I pulled off on Mulholland to feel the Merc take the curves like a lumbering behemoth for the last time. I hated that goddamn car. I would get rid of it immediately. A smile spread across my face, and I laughed so hard I had to pull over. Laughter overtook me, turning to tears and back to a deep, silent laughter in my chest again. From relief. From a break in tension. From sheer joy. I was free. Fucking free.

The car was too small to contain me. I got out and sat on the railing, looking over the city, quiet, tearful bursts overtaking me. I looked at my phone, wanting to say something, connect with someone, but I couldn't conceive the words.

When I recognized where I was, I sobered up. I'd kissed Monica for the first time there. I felt a stabbing twinge in my twisted balls. Oh God, I could have her. I could own her. She could be mine, without hesitation or reservation. Mine. The relief turned into excitement.

I looked at the time. I'd have to wait.

Thinking of Monica, I got calm and focused on my phone.

***

To: Matt.reynolds@harrywinston.com
CC: KristenK@drazeninc.com
Fr: Jon@drazeninc.com

SUBJECT: open a new account

Matt —

Long time.
I need a favor. I need a diamond navel bar. Not a ring. The other kind. Platinum with a 1.25 to 1.375 carat stone. As perfect as you have on hand. Can you deliver it to the east side before noon tomorrow?
Address to come. Let me know.

J Drazen.

***

To: KristenK@drazeninc.com
Fr: Jon@drazeninc.com

SUBJECT: Kevin Wainwright/Faulkner Coal Mine

KK –

Ivan Sinchot is on the board at the L.A. Mod. I need him on the
phone first thing. I want to buy Kevin Wainwright's piece from
Eclipse. All documentation. All copyrights. All assets, period.
Do it through the Ibiza trust, immediately. Drop everything.

-JD

***

My finger hovered over Monica's number. I wanted to talk to her.
No. I didn't want to hear her talk. I wanted to hear her
scream my name. Hours. I wanted her for hours, and time was
one thing I didn't have. I had real business in San Francisco
that couldn't wait, and I had to break it off with Sharon if I
was going to be honest. I texted my pilot, Jacques, telling him
I was on my way.
I looked out over the city, feeling as though I owned it.
Beautiful goddess, when I get back, you are mine.

***

SHARON

JONATHAN

Having lots of money beat the alternatives, for sure. But having a plane didn't mean more privacy. It meant less, because everyone on board was there to serve me. I ended up in the bathroom taking care of the dead weight at the bottom of my balls, as if I'd taken a 727 like everyone else. On my mind was Monica, our first night, when we were so sore and tired I didn't think we'd have another go. She came out of the bathroom, naked, her dark hair a mess, mascara and lipstick worn to nothing. I sat on the edge of the bed waiting for her. She kneeled in front of me, looking up with those big, black eyes. Without a word, she kissed my dick, licking up the shaft, bringing the blood with her until it got hard again.

"Jesus, really?" I'd said.

"It's been eighteen months since I had sex. It might be another eighteen months before I do it again. I'm stocking up."

I'd laughed. I did that a lot with her. I pulled her up, sitting her on my lap, her back to me and my fingers between her legs and on her breast. Since she was stocking up and I thought

I'd never see her again, I fucked her hard, bouncing her on top of me while our hands met between our legs. We connected, feeling each other sliding together. When her back arched, she lost her balance, and we wound up on the floor, laughing, her on her stomach and me coming at her from behind. She turned her head, and I saw the pleasure in her face, her eyes rolling up. She was a gasping, moaning mess, crying and begging for release without being asked.

In the tiny closet of a bathroom on my six-seater plane, my imagination replayed her brown eyes looking up at me while she took my cock in her mouth, then her lips saying *please please, don't stop* from underneath me...My use for the bathroom concluded soon after.

I texted Monica a few times, just a couple of pokes to let her know I wasn't running off and to let myself know I was really doing it.

***

Sharon had been exquisite. Attractive, willing, discreet and far away, she'd do what I told her without question, talk to me about anything, and never open her mouth about who she screwed four or five days a month. Exactly what I needed, when I needed it, and I had been the same for her, but in the end, she needed to make a lifestyle out of her sexuality, and I was just a tourist.

I'd texted her when I landed, but I was two hours early thanks to Jacques answering calls during his morning jog and my desire to clean up business before returning to Los Angeles. She didn't expect me until after my meeting, so I figured she wouldn't be in ready position, and we could talk.

She lived on a high floor of one of my buildings by the Embarcadero. When we'd started screwing, she was a wreck from a string of abusive, boundary-free masters who beat or fucked her confidence away, and I was broken from Jessica's complete rejection of my needs. We were two complete disasters trying to teach each other the meaning of safe, sane, consensual kink. Putting her in one of my apartments seemed like the kindest thing to do, considering she was teaching me as much as I was disciplining her.

The lobby was spare, in dark woods and chrome, with an Italian stone tile floor. I nodded to the doorman and went upstairs.

My phone dinged. It was Sharon.

—I'm ready for you, Sir.—

Shit.

Sharon had three ready positions. That confused her initially. I liked a little surprise. I wanted her to choose, and she was used to being told what to do from how she brushed her teeth, to what she wore, to which route she took to the grocery store. Having a choice of ready position was unheard of in her sexual life, which was why Debbie had set us up in the first place.

But I didn't want her in a ready position. I wanted her clothed and ready to talk.

I opened the door. The place was impeccably clean, every inch made of glass and steel. I could never live in such a space. The apartment was too cold and impersonal, but it was easy to rent or sell, and it was just fine for fucking.

The living room was a big open area with a leather sectional and a shag rectangle under a teak coffee table. Sharon had both hands on the low table, palms spread, arms straight. Her ass was in the air, perched on top of a pair of beautiful legs planted in heels high enough to make a lesser woman fall over. Her blond hair hung over her face, and I knew she was watching me in the mirrors and chrome all over the apartment. Besides the stilettos, she was naked. Naked or underwear was her call, unless I stated otherwise. She was a lovely creature, with curves in the right places and smooth skin she carefully maintained.

Normally, depending on my mood and demeanor after travelling, I'd taunt and touch her until she begged, or I'd slap her ass and fuck her without a word.

I held my hand over her ass, because touching it was the first thing I'd usually do, then I stopped myself. I couldn't tease her because I wouldn't finish what that touch would start. Or worse, I would finish it and make the whole thing a hell of a lot worse.

"You can get up, Sharon."

"I'm sorry, Sir?"

"Get dressed."

"Have I displeased you?"

Fuck. Her voice squeaked with nerves. Bad start. I should have told her to be dressed when I texted her. Total miss on my part.

"No, baby. You're fine. We have to talk, and it's hard to do that with your beautiful ass in my face."

I held out my hand and helped her up. Her face was a blank slate of fear. She had no reason to look scared with me. When we met, any implication of my displeasure was greeted by her acceptance of punishment I had no intention of meting out. It wasn't my thing, but history was hard to shake. She held onto my hand, then pulled it toward her mouth. I twisted away and cupped her cheek. Her grey-blue eyes were full of questions, and her lips were pressed tight, not a position I was used to seeing them in.

"Where do you want to go for breakfast?"

"Wherever you like, Sir."

"Can we not play right now?"

Her posture changed from erect to relaxed. "So," she said, "who is she? Or did the wife come to her senses?"

I smiled. She couldn't have dropped character like that two years ago. "Are you going to get dressed or is the whole town getting a look at you?"

***

Jessica hadn't up and left a perfectly happy marriage. This took a year or more for me to sort out. As I'd become more comfortable with my past, and the man I was, I changed. I became sexually dominant and emotionally controlling. I wanted her to submit to me in bed, which she wouldn't have any of. I wanted her body to be available to me more often, which annoyed her. I wanted her to dress for me, even if I wasn't there. I wanted her to do things during the day, when we were apart. Simple things. Touch herself. Roll her sleeves up. Open her legs. Say my name. It made me feel as though we were connected, but she didn't want to play the game, at all. I became frustrated and unsatisfied. We both dug in, and by the time I was willing to cave on both points to keep her, it was too late.

It had been my fault. I had no idea what I was doing. I didn't know what to ask or what I wanted, I only knew I had new ideas, new excitement, new desires. My requests sounded like demands, when they should have been demands that sounded like requests. I became, in two words, a controlling asshole.

To Sharon, however, I was a sweetheart, and through her and Debbie's stories, I learned just how kinky the kinky world was. I learned how her past men had done things and adjusted what I did to suit me and show her a life that wasn't based on fear, where her needs weren't just important but pleasurable for both of us. It was a shame I couldn't work up an emotion outside general tenderness in the two and some years I'd known her.

Sharon chose a place we'd gone to a hundred times before, with coffee handpicked by college graduates, roasted in the sun only during working hours, trucked in on fuel-efficient vehicles, and made onsite with organic water.

She had her hair tied back with a black velvet twist I'd used to bind her any number of times. No doubt she wore it on purpose. She was used to getting by on her looks and had little to recommend her in the way of conversational skills, but she wasn't stupid. She leaned on her elbows over her skinny latte.

"So?"

"So." I sipped my black coffee. "I wanted to tell you what you've meant to me. You helped me define things I thought had no definition. You've had a big part in making me whole again. I want to thank you for that."

"You never answered my question. The wife or someone else?"

Our relationship was built on honesty and trust but not on fidelity. She'd been on the lookout for a more permanent, full-time Dom, and I'd been searching for what I wanted out of a woman at all. "Both," I said.

"The wife's going to share? I thought she was vanilla?"

"No. Jessica's not going to share, but she did almost get me in the sack. I resisted."

"No *way*! And you turned her down? Why?"

Sharon was rapt. My life's dramas always interested her, yet she'd never betrayed a confidence. "Because I just didn't want her. Honestly. Just didn't. And also, there's someone I promised myself to, at least for the time being."

"Tell me."

"I probably shouldn't."

"What does she look like?"

I shrugged. "Nothing special."

"Oh, please."

I slipped my hand into hers and squeezed it. "You going to be okay without me?"

"You only show up once a month, and you're too gentle anyway."

"Without the tasks and the discipline and knowing I'm there. Are you going to be okay?"

"I think so."

"No assholes."

She took my hand in both of hers and looked me in the eye. "No assholes."

"The apartment. Do you want it?"

"I have some modeling things coming up. I'll pay you for it." I cocked my head at her. She knew what that place cost. "Installment plan."

"Fine."

"Is she short? Tall? How old?"

There is nothing like a woman's curiosity about other women. She'd never imply or even admit to herself she felt an ounce of competition between herself and Monica, yet she had to know so she could compare herself and decide if she was okay with it.

"I meet a lot of beautiful girls," I said. "She's...I don't know. The first time I talked to her, in my office, she was a waitress at my hotel. I looked at her, trying to figure out why she looked so tangible, so *present*. Every curve looked exactly right. Even her skin is this perfect color...Not even color. The texture of it. I wanted to touch it like I'd never wanted to touch anything before. She saw me looking, and she stood with her hands on her hips, daring me to get an eyeful. No fear. She filled that fucking room." I sipped my coffee. "She took my breath away. I was too stunned to even ask her out."

"So?" Sharon might have been watching the last fifteen minutes of a Lifetime movie, her attention was so focused.

"So I got her a job at the Stock, where Debbie works. I figured she could check her out, tell me if I was crazy."

"So smart, you. What did she say?"

"You know Debbie. She won't rest until everyone's happily coupled off but her."

I sensed rue in Sharon's smile. I rested my hand on her forearm. "You'll find someone, baby."

She shrugged. "Maybe. I don't think it matters. Can you stay for one last fuck?"

I checked my watch as if it was a possibility. "Got a meeting with Tim LaShaun from District 34. Then a tenant's advocacy group that wants my head on a stick. More bullshit tomorrow and the next."

She nodded. I always had at least that much bullshit when I came to San Francisco, but things was different, and she knew it. There wouldn't be one last fuck. I'd done it. I'd come out unscathed and true to my word. I was less confident about Sharon. She had a way of putting a nice face on everything until she decided the pain was too much to bear.

We parted outside. I gave her a hug and a kiss on the cheek. I felt that relief again, but unlike the previous night, when I'd walked out on Jessica, it felt less like getting hit in the head by a two-by-four.

My phone rang as I put Sharon in a cab.

"Hi, Debbie," I answered as I handed the valet my ticket. "Speak of the devil. I was just with Sharon."

As usual, she wasted no time getting to the point. "Jessica met Monica last night?"

"Correct."

"She came here and insisted on sitting at her station."

Ugly. It was just like Jessica to highlight any class difference she could tease out. Having Monica serve her would be a way to humiliate her with a smile.

Debbie continued, "I don't expect you to do anything about it. Except your wife—"

"Ex-wife."

"She said something to Monica. I don't know what, but now the girl looks like she's been slapped."

My fingers got ice cold. Jessica could have said a hundred things, secrets she could have revealed or implied. A million half-truths. Without a man to lean on, she was a cornered animal. I'd forgotten how dangerous she was when I was busy choosing another woman over her.

"Did you ask Monica?" I asked.

"She won't repeat it."

Apparently, my beautiful goddess was also a woman of honor. "I'll call her."

"She's working the floor, so her phone is off. Fix it, please. I don't like it. The power trip. It's sneaky."

"I will, Debbie. I will."

I hung up. My car came, and I parked it around the corner to give myself a minute to think. What did Jessica know? Everything. What was she willing to share? Or imply? Or use? I had no idea. I knew for sure I wasn't ready to share everything about my past with Monica, not a word or deed I didn't have to, because I'd lose her. Any woman would run for the hills.

I texted Monica before I drove away.

—Can you call me?—

***

When I got out of my first meeting, she still hadn't called. She'd gotten the text, so her silence was intentional.

If I were her, what would I do?

Whatever Jessica had said, I'd be finding out if it was true. So I had to make the investigation impossible to complete. That meant moving Rachel, touching base with each sister, Deirdre especially, and stressing their silence. And Thomas. And the hospital. And dad, who would laugh in my face. And...Fuck. There were too many fires to put out. Too many pieces to move across the chessboard.

I put my phone in my pocket.

It occurred to me that I'd longed for Jessica because she knew all the ugliness of my past. I didn't have to reveal a thing to her. I didn't have to bear the uncertainty and loneliness of wondering what someone thought of me. But if she loved me through it, couldn't someone else? Couldn't someone else keep a secret or ten? Maybe, but I was getting ahead of myself. I was letting my excitement get ahead of my sense. I had to finish up here and get back to LA without panicking.

I made my way to my meeting with the tenant's rights group. That bunch would use that information to take me down, even if I gave them what they wanted. I had to deal with Jessica at some point, no matter what, unless I was willing to live without intimacy the way I wanted it. Or I would risk losing Monica before we even started.

***

Rachel.

Do people like you ever have wishes, Jonathan?
What does that mean? People like me?
People who have everything. Was there ever something you wanted but could only wish for?

***

JONATHAN

I hated the word *festooned*.

Festooned implied some kind of old-world family dancing around with ribbons, draping them over lamps and doorways, catching the flowers as they fell out of their hair. It brought to mind musical theater and swaying skirts. It felt *Swiss Family Robinson. Mary Poppins. The Waltons.* Good night, Jon-boy.

Despite the sour taste in the front of my tongue and the bitter one in back, *festooned* was the only word that suited the house on this, the day of my engagement party. I wanted to drink far more than I had. I wanted to take that bottle of Jameson's I knew my mother hid under her bathroom vanity and sit in a corner to finish it. I wanted to suck it dry. But I didn't do that anymore. When I drank, I held a glass and sipped until the ice melted, never finishing before. Then I waited and eventually got another. I hadn't been drunk since I was sixteen.

And if I did drink that bottle? Who would care but my fiancé, Jessica? Or more to the point, whose opinion did I value besides hers? Who else did I serve?

She wanted this event, and she got it. I couldn't deny her anything, and really, it wasn't such a big deal to throw a party. It was nothing to gather a team of people from Hotel A to *festoon* my parent's Palisades house, send invitations to the right people, and make sure there was food. My staff were experts at managing women with exquisite taste, such as my bride-to-be. It was no burden to me whatsoever.

The burden was having the engagement at my father's house. The burden was explaining to him that the wedding would be at the my future in-law's residence in Venice, and his presence was not requested.

There were reasons for all of it, of course, spite not being the least of them. I understood spite, even enjoyed it on occasion, poured over cold cubes of guilt with a chaser of regret. But this spite was too old and too ugly to enjoy.

"There you are," my mother's voice came from behind me. I'd been looking out toward the yard, watching subsets of staff ready it for the flood of people. "Have you seen Jess?"

"She's out with my sisters getting her feet and fingers done. Something tasteful, I'm sure. No need to worry."

Mom slipped her hands over my shoulders, her hands brushing the fabric free of some imaginary lint. "Are you happy?"

"Why do you ask?"

"You've seemed down. Is it Jessica?"

"No."

"The thing with your father?" Mom didn't look concerned as much as benign. She'd perfected that look of harmlessness over forty years, and she wore it well under light makeup and a strawberry blonde chignon.

"Yes."

"He's come to terms with it."

"Is the bar up? I need a drink."

She looped her arm into mine and we walked outside.

***

My father hadn't ever actually come to terms with anything in his life, ever. He sat and waited until opportunities presented themselves. He was utterly non-aggressive in the way a cat is utterly still outside a mouse hole, waiting for the rodent to either forget he was trapped or get hungry enough to risk everything and leave.

The party setup was going smoothly, people in tuxedos and black dresses gadding about with purpose. The hedges had been trimmed, the tennis court locked. The pool had been cleaned, repainted and decorated with floating flowers. No one asked me a goddamn thing about anything and I liked it that way. The bartender, an actor from the looks of him, was setting up glasses in neat rows. Behind him, the majesty of the Pacific Ocean stretched into a haze where sea met sky.

"He told me he understood," Mom said, continuing a conversation she assumed I wanted to have. "Business deals sometimes go bad and someone gets hurt."

"It's fine, ma."

"You should talk to him about it."

"Hey," I said to the bartender. "Two Jameson's, rocks."

"I'm not having any," Mom said.

"They're both for me."

She smiled and punched my arm. "Jon. Always the joker. Listen to me. This radio silence with your father isn't productive. I mean, he did agree to have the engagement here."

"You insisted."

"To save him embarrassment. This thing with him has put me in the middle and to be truthful, it's stressful."

She knew how to feel stress, my mother. The management of anxiety was an art form with her, necessitating the use of a cocktail of medications and hospitalizations when she misjudged her secret alcohol intake. Poor Mom. Really. A willing captive in a house as big as an island nation.

It was my turn to flick an imaginary piece of lint off her shoulder. "He took my future in-laws for everything, blew a chunk of it and passed a few million back to them. Not enough for them to get a decent lawyer."

"It was twelve years ago and it was a legitimate business deal."

"Legal. It was legal. Not legitimate."

Despite earlier denials, she took the glass of whiskey, holding it but not putting it to her lips, as if it was a prop. I remembered she drank wine in public and whiskey in private. I was getting muddled already.

"I know they're your family now, the Carneses. But don't forget where you came from, young man."

As if I ever could.

***

The last family party my father and I had attended together had been seven years earlier. Sheila's birthday had an unfortunate proximity to Christmas, so every one of her birthday parties became Christmas parties. Her house in Palos Verdes perched on the edge of a sheer drop to the ocean. For a mile in each direction, a beach as wide as a sidestreet ribboned at the base of the cliff. But toward the end of that year, the beach disappeared under rushing tides as it rained for twenty days straight.

Children toddled underfoot, with nannies running bent-kneed behind them. Extended family on top of extended family, most drunk or on their way there, myself included, even at sixteen. I did what I wanted, like all my friends. Nothing could happen to us that money couldn't fix, so no one paid attention.

I had no self-control at that point. I was a loose cannon of temperamental fits, drunken rages, and risky behavior. The last incident had been driving my father's new Maserati into South Gate to drag my friend Gordon out of a meth house. I'd thrown him into the driver's side and hit the gas from the passenger's side to wake his sorry ass out of a stupor. We'd sideswiped his dealer's Escalade, four-thousand-dollars' worth, and in the end, Gordon had gone right back to using, but my addiction to nearly dying had been sated for a month, at least.

Then, the week before Christmas, Sheila's birthday. Los Angles had already had twenty-two inches of rain since school started. There was a rumor Death Valley would have a once-in-a-lifetime bloom, come spring. My friends and I were planning a road trip in Charles's Hummer just to mow our path over fields of poppies.

I was drunk already, bullshitting with my cousin Arthur over which Ivy League schools we were going to stroll into. Which had the best clubs, where the legacies were. Arthur was a douchebag. The last time I'd driven down Sunset with him, he leaned out of his BMW to make some noise at a girl, which was bad enough. But when she flipped him the bird he shouted, "Man, I bet there's some guy out there so tired of fucking you."

"Arthur, really?" I felt like getting out and apologizing to her, but the light turned green and we were gone.

"What, Jon? Look at her. All legs and shit. Fuck her."

That was the last time I went out with Arthur. But at a family party, as long as we kept to schools and baseball, I could hold a conversation with him.

Sheila's party graduated from family thing to some kind of pre-Christmas fuckall event, and the kitchen got crowded. I was less and less inclined to move. People I knew came in and out, most not related to me at that point, and aunts and uncles kissed me goodbye and left.

I don't even know what I was drinking. A bong went around. It was lead crystal and totally illegal, even if the bud wasn't, and the liquid inside was chartreuse absinthe.

Just because.

The movement of the party shifted down the hall, through the library and into the living room, where I saw my father was still there.

And Rachel had shown up.

***

Was there ever something you wanted, but could only wish for,
Jonathan?
I wish I wasn't raised by crazy people.
Something for the future. That you want, but don't think you'll get.
Yes, I—
Don't tell me. That'll ruin it.

***

Jessica was nowhere to be found. She didn't answer my texts
or calls. Margie, who had taken her out for the "girl thing"
with three other sisters, said my fiancé had left the spa in her
Mercedes the hour before.

"Did she have an accident?"

"I don't know little brother," Margie said, grabbing a glass
of wine before the first guest arrived. "She seemed fine. The
usual."

"What does that mean?" I felt a stab of anger. Seven sisters.
A couple were bound to dislike my wife.

"Charming and polite. Warm, even. But not."

"Howdy!" Leanne came across the empty backyard, grabbing a glass as soon as the bartender poured it. The emerald of
her dress brought out the fire engine in her hair. "You should
see Jess's nails. She got a French with an airbrush. So cute."

"Did you see her out front?" I asked.

"Nope. Are those the cufflinks you're wearing?" Leanne
fixed the flowers in her hair by the reflection in the window.
She wanted to make clothes, so Dad had bought her a factory.
Another money-losing proposition. Next to Deirdre, the still
devout, chronically depressed Irish poet, she was the most cre-
ative in the family.

"No," I said. "I just wore these to offend you."

"He wants to know how Jessica looked." Margie said.

"Cool and collected. She's a rock, you know." Leanne
squeezed my cheeks. "You did good."

Leanne, who was habitually single at twenty-six because she was a workaholic, had no business judging, even when I agreed with her.

***

I was fifteen, and Rachel was a year and a half older when we began seeing each other, if that's what you could call it. Discretion was absolutely necessary, so she didn't come to any family parties. I didn't want her near my father, period. End of. She knew why. I knew why. No one else did. Her old affair with my father when she was too young and impressionable to know better was a secret bought and paid for with jewelry and electronics. I kept it for her because she wanted it that way, and though I would have loved to tell the world about what kind of animal my father was, the understanding between myself and a few of my sisters, was that Mom would break into a hundred pieces if what she knew in her heart was confirmed. My father was, so far, the luckiest son of a bitch in the world.

Rachel and I were rarely seen in public together unless she went to a Loyola ballgame I pitched, or if I happened to show up at a play she was in. It was hard to stay away from her, but necessary. We didn't talk about a future past the possibility that we could attend the same college, provided she got a scholarship.

We met in my car, late at night after Mom was passed out. Dad was gone often and he would have let me out the front door anyway. The staff didn't care, or expected no less: another irresponsible rich brat, in a society full of them, slipping out to debauch himself on school nights.

Rachel had a harder time of it. She had a tough home life. Her stepfather went into a controlling fits, locking her and her mother in the house at night. The windows were barred and the deadbolts had inside keys he slept with. In her closet, Rachel found a trapdoor to the crawlspace under the house. I met her on the corner. Seeing her walk even a block in the dark in that neighborhood twisted my stomach in knots, every time. I never got used to it. Usually, when she got into the car, I laughed from released tension and the sight of cobwebs in her hair.

She attended Marlborough on a hefty financial aid package which was still a stretch for her parents, and was required to maintain a GPA of 3.75 or face the budget cuts and substandard educational opportunities of the LAUSD. She was in the home stretch. Smart, diligent, studious, and yes, beautiful; she would be the first in her family to attend a top school and get a medical degree. I'd have followed her anywhere. Business schools were a dime a dozen, and Dad would buy me entry to the university of my choice, even if I never told him why the choice was made. In this case, Rachel and I chose University of Pennsylvania and crossed our fingers, she for Perelman School of Medicine, and I for Wharton a year later. It was Ivy League, which was easy for me, and hard for her.

All this meant she didn't have the time or permission to drive around in my Mercedes, or run into hotel rooms with me. But we were young, and infatuated, and on the cusp of freedom, or in her case, death.

***

What do you mean by "wish" then, Rachel?
Like, hope you get something you know is impossible, but hope anyway.
I wish I could be with you like a normal person.
What's normal to someone like you?

***

The backyard buzzed with activity. Fiona, never one to miss an opportunity to invite Deirdre's scorn, had managed to book psychics, tarot card readers, crystal healers and a hypnotist for the cocktail hour.

The black baby grand had been brought onto the patio, and the four musicians Dad had plucked from some music school in central LA set up stands and instruments. Piano, two violins, and cello. Except the first violinist wasn't tuning a violin. She was tuning a viola. Hardly worth making a fuss over, except she was stunning, with full lips and long, dark hair. She had to be five-ten in flat feet, with a chin that pointed upwards as if daring the world to hit her on the jaw.

"She's magnificent, no?"

My father's voice beside me, admiring a girl who was probably in high school. I looked away quickly.

"Jail bait, dad. Ever hear of it?" I turned to face him. In his late fifties, he was still a good-looking guy. His red hair had turned completely silver five years earlier, and stayed fully attached to his head. The girls loved him. And when I said girls, I meant just that. Girls.

"You're avoiding me. I was looking for some common ground."

"Uh-huh." I didn't know where to start with him. Common-ground wise, we had Rachel. That was awkward enough. I glanced around. We were relatively alone, a situation Mom never let slide if she could.

He spoke quietly, barely moving his lips. "You never stop wanting them that age. Every man fantasizes about the dew on the flower."

"You're sick."

"Were you not just looking at that girl? She can't be a day over fifteen. On the evening of your engagement, no less. It's time to accept reality, son. The need is biological. You can fight it your whole life if you want to, but it will be a fight."

He looked like he'd wanted to say that to me for a long time. Like it was some kind of big talk every man gives their son, and it had been denied him by my avoidance and Mom's intervention.

"We aren't having a meeting of the minds on underage girls."

"Except the one," he said as if we had some delightful shared history.

"I'm going to need you to stay away from my wife, and if there are children, especially if there are children—"

He got that look. The one like he was being electrocuted. It was hard rage directed forward. I'd only seen it once before, days after I found out what he was and I saw him touching Theresa's arm when he spoke to her.

"Do not ever presume that I don't have boundaries, son."

Much as an animal won't shit where they eat, he'd never touched any of my sisters, but when I flew at him I didn't know that. We may have been evenly matched the day he laid a chaste touch on Theresa, but at my engagement party, I was older, taller, and less fearful.

"You will never be alone with my children," I said. "Those are *my* boundaries." I took a gulp of my whiskey. Too much. The drink would never last if I kept doing that. But I needed to do more than let the liquid touch my lips when I stared at him over the glass.

"I wanted to just elope somewhere far away," I said, seeing Mom coming up behind him, "so there would be no problems with Jessica's family. But it wasn't possible. I'm sorry you've been insulted in the process. Truly."

He smirked, because he knew the kinder tone and change of subject must have come for one reason. He and I had come to blows after Rachel's accident, and I'd taken a handful of pills. Mom didn't let us alone in the same room if she could avoid it. Over the past seven years, she'd run a pretty tight interference. I had to admire her aversion to conflict. It had kept her in a state of blissful, drunken ignorance that my sisters and I had sworn to protect until death.

Dad took the opportunity to clap me on the back just as the string quartet started warming up.

"No worries, son. No worries. It was just business. Can't win at it and make friends, too."

I smiled, not mentioning the tens of millions in payoff money that had drained him to the point where only shady deals kept him afloat. Nope. It was all smiles when Mom reached us. Dad put his arm around her and I made it a point to shake his hand like a gentleman so she would enjoy the rest of the evening.

"Jonny! Come over here?"

"Come on!"

"This is perfect!"

It was the sound of a gaggle of sisters. Four rushed up in green dresses and varying shades of strawberry chignon. Margie, Sheila, Leanne, and Theresa. Their voices became a cheering chatter.

"You have to see the hypnotist."

"He's going to relax you."

"You're too tense."

"A teepee and a wigwam!"

"It'll only take a second."

The drink was taken from my hand and I felt myself being pulled to a guy in a fedora and handlebar moustache sitting by one of our chaise lounges.

"Hang on, hang on..." I held my hands up in surrender.

"What?"

"It's fun!"

"Chicken."

"Bok bok bok."

They were beautiful, each one of my older sisters. A huge pain in my ass, each in a different way, but all precious. And annoying.

"I need to use the restroom. If he relaxes me too much I'm going to have a problem, if you know what I mean. That's all."

Margie, the oldest and most practical, who didn't believe in anything but money and death, took charge, spinning me by my shoulders. "Go. Then you're back here or we're dragging you out for a crystal cleansing."

I walked to the house, making a point of not looking at the stunning brunette plucking her viola. Not easy. She had the kind of face one stared at. But I glanced over, and there was Dad, talking to her, leaning over in a way that seemed respectful and dignified, getting her comfortable. I wondered if he did it to spite me, then remembered he simply and shamelessly liked fucking girls too young to drink legally. It had nothing to do with me. Which meant I'd be unable to get him away from her. I couldn't say, 'Okay Dad, you're right, high school girls are hot. Now can you step away?' because then he'd take her to bed for sure. I couldn't try and cut in or he'd make a light hearted competition of our pursuit. And I couldn't cross-check him through the windows or I'd ruin my own party, and I'd have to explain to my fiancée why I was protecting the honor of an underage girl I'd only glanced at.

I got past them and into the house. I needed another drink, but my excuse to Margie had been real. On the way to the hall bathroom, I spotted the pianist from the quartet. A blonde with faded acne and an odd, melancholy confidence.

"Excuse me," I said.

"Yeah?"

"Your friend? On the viola?"

"Monica?"

"Tell her no flirting with the guests or hosts. Understand?"

Her look went from offense to curiosity, as she craned her neck to see past the sitting room windows. The set up for the quartet was just about visible.

"Oh, crap."

"I'm serious."

"She's not like that really," her words ran together. "I mean she's just started seeing my brother, but she's not a flirt like that at all. She's barely even friendly."

Caught between the desire to know more and the desire to run away, I simply walked quickly and rudely down the hall before I heard another word about that woman.

Girl.

***

I never let myself truly fall for Rachel. I'd always felt bad about that. I'd trapped her, protecting myself from that moment I'd see her and my father in the same room. Unfortunately, all that guarded emotion didn't pay off. At Sheila's party, Rachel had shown up with Theresa, and Dad was still there. When I saw them together, I felt like my spine was being ripped out. She was giving him what-for with her finger extended and mouth demanding something through gritted teeth and intense, burning eyes.

He took whatever verbal abuse she was dishing out with the serious air of a guy who didn't give a shit. This man was impossible to understand unless you saw him work a room, his uncanny appeal, the way he didn't look like a fifty year-old man in a party full of kids. The way he melted into any situation. The magnetism I never understood was illustrated over and over again, even as he refused advances when Mom was around, and always left open a maybe as soon as she turned her back.

As I got closer to them, I got disproportionately angry. Rachel wasn't supposed to be there. That was the rule, and it was in place because seeing her in the vicinity of my father made me consider patricide with a cold, collected calm that scared me.

My peripheral vision closed in on her as I navigated the crowd. It's possible the multiple bong hits were making me paranoid. There was zero danger of her falling into his clutches that, or any night. But I didn't want him to know I was just short of loving her. I didn't want him to have information he could use, because he'd use it to hurt me. He'd pulled strings to keep Margie from a man he found threatening, destroying a law firm rather than have her work there. He'd do it to me, but as the only male of eight children, the damage would come faster and I'd fare far worse.

"Rachel," I said when I reached her. Her pale brown eyes were tear-streaked, and her beautiful mouth cut into a line of rage. "Come on, let's go."

My father smiled as if I was rescuing him from an embarrassing incident.

And that was the last I remembered of that night.

***

On our backs, in the grass of Elysian Park, where my family would never find us, Rachel and I stared at the clouds. She liked to wonder what it would be like to be me. She thought I had not a worry in the world. Yes, my father was a fucking sociopath, but he didn't stick his fingers inside me like hers had, and he didn't scream and hit and lock me in the house like her stepfather had. And for me, whatever I endured would end when my trust fund spread its legs at twenty-one. For her, the light at the end of the tunnel had not appeared.

"Do you wish for things you can't buy?" she asked.

I looked over at her. Blades of grass sat in the foreground of my vision, slashing her face, which was turned to me. Her eyes were tobacco brown, wide and light, catching the sun inside them. "You're fascinated with money," I said.

"I think I am." She smiled. "It's made you different, you know. You're fearless. It's exciting, kind of. Watching you is like watching someone who's really, truly free."

I laughed. I never felt free in my life.

"What do you wish for?" I asked. "Besides money."

"You make me sound like a golddigger."

"You are, but you're terrible at it. I think a few more years and you'll be sleeping with the right guy."

She flung herself on top of me and pinched my sides. I laughed and rolled her over until I had her pinned.

"Tell me what you wish for, and if it's any part of my body, your wish will come true at the Regency Hotel in forty minutes."

She giggled and turned her face to the sunlight. "Free, Jonathan. I wish to be free."

I unpinned one of her shoulders to pluck a seeded dandelion out of the grass.

"Blow," I said, holding the white puffball in front of her.

She blew hard, and the seeds went into my face. We laughed, and blew the rest of the seeds off together, wishing her free from the constraints of her family and her scarcity. They floated away on their sinuous parachutes, like little messengers to God, saying take me, take me, take me. Set me free.

***

"You're mine," Leanne said, yanking me out into the backyard.

"Did anyone hear from Jessica yet?"

"She stopped to get you something."

"Pepto bismol, I hope."

A few early birds gathered around the bar. I'd be on call for congratulating and handshaking soon, so I hoped I could get hypnotized into a state of blissful relaxation in five minutes or less. Didn't seem possible.

Theresa, standing with the gaggle of green, waved me over to the man in a tweed jacket and handlebar moustache.

We shook hands.

"David Mesmer's the name. I hear you're a little tense?"

"Mesmer, huh? Any relation?"

"Great grandfather. I fell into the profession. Lie down right here."

The sky was clear blue and sunless as the day darkened into night. I felt ridiculous lying on a chaise in a formal suit. I felt vulnerable and scrutinized by four of my seven sisters. I feared I'd miss Jessica's arrival if I wasn't by the door and if any of my friends saw me getting hypnotized the ribbing would break a bone.

"Let's get this over with," I said.

"Said like a truly anxious man. Can you focus your mind on what's making you tense? I'm going to count backwards from ten."

The string quartet keyed up and began with Mendelssohn. Very nice, even for a group of teenagers. Despite being from the gifted school, I hadn't expected much, especially not from the viola. No one could be that beautiful and talented at the same time. But her beauty carried to her playing, because as David counted back from ten, I didn't hear a goddamn thing past five except the viola as if there was not another instrument on the planet.

***

The rain on the night of Sheila's party was near blinding.

"Stop it!" Rachel shouted, snapping away the jacket I tried to hold over her head. "I want to get wet, that's why I came into the rain. To get wet!"

I tossed the jacket to the side. "You came out here because I'm taking you home."

"You're crazy!"

Drunk as I'd been that night, I took in the conversation as a cold, sober observer. On the night it actually happened, alcohol had blacked me out. I remembered nothing after Rachel saw my face and stood up. My memory of the events of that night ended there, and were retold to me by the media and my parents. The hypnosis was like watching a movie in my own point of view.

"I am sick of this," she shouted. "I'm sick of you wanting to know where I am all the time. Sick of it. You're a control freak. You're worse than my stepdad, do you know that?"

I knew I was getting hypnotized. I knew Franz Mesmer's great grandson had counted from ten and my body was at my engagement party, and I also knew the movie was about to play the part where I lost someone I cared about.

"What the hell did you think you were doing in there?" I growled. Though I felt all the panic and fear I felt that night, I was also my older self, who knew how it all ended.

Calm down. Get control. My older self spoke to my younger self urgently, as if it could change anything.

"What's going to happen when I go to college? You going to tell me who to talk to from here? Should I keep a log of what I wear? Well I won't. Nothing. No more." Rachel's brown hair was soaked. She'd run out in a light sweater, leaving her jacket and purse behind.

"What were you saying to him?" I yelled.

"You really want to know?"

I stepped forward. I was already six feet tall, an intimidating presence in the class, and in front of a young woman in the rain.

She stepped back. "I'm not going to get enough to go to Penn, so J. Declan Drazen's coughing it up. Every fucking dime, or I'm telling everyone what a sick bunch of fucks you are."

She and I were open about what a sick bunch of fucks we were. We even laughed about it sometimes, but I'd always felt like she was talking about my parents. This time, it sounded like I was included. It sounded like she'd be more than happy to take me down as just another sick fuck who bedded her. What had I thought I meant to her? Did she think I'd used her? Or was it the other way around?

"Don't play with him, Rachel. You can't win."

"I'm not playing." She looked more like a grown woman when she uttered those words than ever before. She really meant to tangle with my father.

I took my car keys out. "I'm taking you home."

She stepped back, under the edge of the eave, where the water dripped in fatter, condensed streams. One splashed on her shoulder, but she didn't notice or didn't care.

"I'm sorry." Her voice cracked. "Don't look at me like that. I love you Jay."

"And I'm just one of the sick fucks? Did I ever treat you with anything but respect?"

"There's too much baggage, Jonathan. I want a regular boyfriend."

I froze. What did she mean? Instead of asking her, in my immaturity and drunkenness, I stepped forward again.

You're being menacing. She's going to run…she's going to—

She snapped the car keys from my hand.

"Give me those." I grabbed for them, but my balance was off, and I was slow.

She ran.

I ran after her, but the images got foggy and indistinct.

I was in the driveway, looking for my car.

I was in the house, searching through coat pockets.

I was driving in a shitstorm of rain.

How? What did I miss?

I felt a pain in my shoulder.

I was in the driver's side of the car. It was too dark to make out much more than the outline of the keys. They seemed to stand up sideways in the ignition, defying gravity. My vision swam. Then the keys rotated on the ring, pointing toward the ceiling. Odd.

Creak.

Crunch.

I was on the ground. I heard the beep of the warning signal and saw the beam of a single headlight, but all I saw was a car on its side, ready to fall into the whirling floods of the Pacific Ocean.

It rolled and fell. There was no splash. When I scrambled up to the edge of the cliff, a car was floated in the foaming waters.

I heard her scream.

Rachel.

It had to be. She must have been belted into the passenger side?

But how?

"Rachel!" I yelled. What a ridiculous thing to do. I could barely hear myself.

I dove into the water.

Cold.

I became aware of the viola again, just as I gulped water and felt a stabbing pain in my lungs. The real me, the me at my engagement party, the twenty three-year old who had control of his life, gasped real air and felt water. I was coming out of it.

But the sixteen year-old me woke up to grass tickling my nose. The world swam as if I was riding the teacups at Disney. I opened my eyes. Just in front of me, so close I had no context but a few blades of grass, the dark of the rainy night, and my own nausea, was Rachel's face. She, too had her cheek to the grass. Her eyes glazed over. Her mouth hung open. Her hair stuck to her face in the rain. She blinked, and a tear fell over the bridge of her nose.

Rachel, Rachel, I am sorry.

***

The sound of the full quartet sounded like a philharmonic, and I knew I was out of the hypnosis a second before I bolted straight in my chair. Jessica sat on the edge of the chaise in an ecru dress. The orchid in her hand matched the one in her blonde hair. She must have gotten it for my lapel on the way back from the manicurist. She always thought of everything.

"Jon," she said, taking my hand. "What happened?"

"You have to meet me halfway," grumbled David Mesmer.

"Jonathan," Theresa said. "Let me get you a drink, my God."

The other sister's voices broke into my consciousness. Jessica and I just looked at each other, barely hearing.

"You look *worse*."

"We really need to try the crystal cleansing lady."

"Have the guy with the wine come this way."

"Christ, I think half of Stanford just showed up."

Jessica slipped her hand between mine and tugged. I got up. I pulled her away to a quiet corner between two chest-high planters.

"Are you all right?" she whispered.

"I don't believe in hypnosis," I said.

"Of course not." She pressed the orchid to my lapel and wove a three inch straight pin through it, fastening it to my jacket. Her eyes gazed at me suspiciously and with no little concern. "But you look like you just saw a ghost."

"I remembered that night. Things I hadn't remembered before."

"That night? Jon, really. Which night?"

"The night Rachel died."

She touched my cheek, and I brought my arm around her waist. "Tell me," she said.

I put my lips close to her ear. "She's alive."

"How is that possible?"

"I remember. I woke up in the grass, and she was next to me. Her eyes were open. She blinked."

Nothing about Jessica's expression changed for the first second, and I watched her closely. I needed her to tell me something. Maybe comfort me, or tell me I was wrong. Maybe

I'd missed a shred of evidence that proved what we'd always known. That Rachel was dead and buried and the family tracks covered with six feet of dirt.

She put her hand on my lapel. "You know, this isn't a reliable memory, right?"

"Yes. But I also know it's right. Sure as we're standing here."

"Well then, there's only one way to know for sure." She squeezed my hand and put her lips to my ear. "We'll have to find her."

A streamer floated down from a tree and landed between us, while the sound of the quartet drew my attention back to my engagement party and waiting guests.

***

A VALENTINE FROM JONATHAN
To be read after Sing

The following short was released as a Valentine's Day special for the SubClub.

The story takes place about six weeks after Jonathan's transplant. I tried to stick it in the beginning of the book, and it didn't work. Then I tried to stick it in as a memory, and that didn't work either, so here it is...

JONATHAN

I'd taken just about everything in my life for granted. Money, intelligence, women, family, but mostly my health. I protected it easily, worked through the bumps in the road, and exercised when I felt like it. I ate what I wanted, when I wanted, unless it was spicy. Then I just avoided it.

"You have a heart biopsy today," my wife mumbled, her face buried in her pillow.

I brushed her hair behind her ear. I was sitting up in bed, and I had been for a few hours. I didn't inherit my heart from a sleeper apparently, so I still stayed up half the night. I was used to that. What I wasn't used to was being so weak I couldn't be out of bed for more than a few hours at a time.

I hated spicy food I'd loved before. I had a strange urge to run, as if the road called to me. I couldn't drink enough juice. All that was supposedly normal, as a rogue group of cells were peeling off the heart and sticking to my organs, but I felt way past the age when I should be discovering things about myself.

"I'm not going," I said.

"Like hell."

"I feel fine. I'm only supposed to get the biopsies if they think I'm rejecting."

She got up on her elbows. "Jonathan, let's not do this again."

I could see the tops of her breasts as they fell into her white tank. We hadn't made love since I'd gotten out of the hospital. We were afraid, both of us. I didn't even know who we were sometimes.

"Let's not then," I said.

She rolled onto her back. The February chill always managed to get through the old windows, and the result was hard nipples pushing through her tank. She was still, as always, magnificent, and I felt a forgotten stirring.

"I'll go with you," she said. "Then we can get something to eat, and you'll be back for a nap."

"You're in the studio today."

"I'll cut out. Eddie can reschedule."

My hand, as if it had a mind of its own, brushed her nipple with the backs of my fingers. It bent under my fingers four times, then my thumb stayed, rolling it. Her eyes closed, and her mouth opened. She was the same, sensitive as a raw nerve ending, but she wouldn't let me touch her until recently. I'd satisfied her twice since then, but we couldn't do more together because of the nagging, overwhelming fear.

"You are not to reschedule again or ever," I said, pinching the nipple.

"You have to go for the biopsy." She groaned.

I was hard. Very hard. "No, I don't." I yanked at her panties. "Take these off."

She looked at me for a second, her brown eyes big as coffee cups. She grabbed at the sides of her underwear and wiggled out of them. She'd started gaining weight back, and though the sickly gauntness was gone, her hip bones still jutted out too far under her skin, and the space between her thighs was too apparent. Getting something to eat probably wasn't a bad idea, except I wasn't getting another fucking biopsy.

She was still on her back, all hard nipples and hidden cunt. I didn't know if I could. Physically, I had been cleared for fucking, but I still didn't feel right. "Legs spread, knees up. Come on. Let me see."

She did as she was told, as always, and I slid my hand down her belly, past her triangle, to her waiting lips. She gasped.

"You're fucking soaked. I never met a woman who needed to fuck so bad."

"Get the biopsy. God, please." Her head was thrown back. "I'll suck your cock right now."

"You're not using sex to bribe me are you?"

"I am, I am."

Good, great God she needed a spanking. Six months ago, I would have welted her for doing what she was doing, but I didn't think I could take any kind of intensity. I knew my heart wouldn't pound since the vagus nerve had been cut, but having her clit under my fingers without feeling a racing heart as accompaniment to my desire was disconcerting. I felt dead at the same time as I felt on the precipice of life.

I took my fingers from her and glossed her lips with her juice. She opened her mouth and sucked on my fingers. I was about to spontaneously combust, but I couldn't. Not yet. I was still not myself, still afraid, like a child. I was ashamed of my fear but not ashamed enough to conquer it.

I put my hand between her legs again, sliding inside her, up to her clit, and back. Her hand stroked between my thighs. I squeezed her clit, and she arched her back, then I touched the tip of it.

She gasped. "Let me suck you. Please. I'll go slow."

"No." I flattened my fingers against her, pushed two into her cunt, and moved her clit with my palm. I pulled my fingers out again and back. "Look at me."

She opened her eyes, and I leaned down to kiss her. Her mouth tasted like cunt, and her tongue tasted like morning.

"Say my name."

"Jonathan."

I put three fingers in her and drew them out. She squeaked.

"Jonathan."

"Come." I moved faster, harder.

"Jonathan. Oh. Jonathan." She arched her back, pushing her arms over her, crying out my name. Music, but with half an orchestra.

***

The technician breezed in wearing scrubs and a full suit of medical detachment. She was young and attractive, with no makeup and straight brown hair pulled back in an efficient ponytail. I had the best team in the world, and they treated me like any other patient. I guessed that was what I was paying them for.

"We're going in through the arm today," she said through her mask.

"That's what the doctor said."

"Are we doing the nitrous?"

Jesus fucking Christ, save me from the habitual pluralization of experience. "Nope."

"It's going to be uncomfortable." Her tag said Fran. A bland name. It suited her.

"We'll manage." God, I was cranky.

Fran moved her tray of sharp things in front of her, and I laid out my arm. My first biopsy had been through the jugular vein. I suspected this would feel less invasive, more like a walk in the park while a tube snaked through my body. The swab was cold on my skin, and I went into meat mode, where I went someplace else in my mind while I was treated like a side of beef.

"So," she said, beginning the small talk that preceded painful invasions, "we're married, I see." She pointed at my ring. "What are we doing for Valentine's Day?"

I didn't answer.

"Mister Drazen? Are you okay?"

I think the word "you," as opposed to "we," woke me faster than the real concern in her voice. "Today's the fourteenth?"

"Yup," she said, dicking around with her plastic and metal tinker toys.

"Shit."

"We're going to the Getty Center. They have this romantic dinner prix fix on the patio. They put candles on the fountain, and they have a really nice string quartet."

"Shit," I repeated. "I forgot."

"Oh. Well. Maybe we can still get it together in time? Going in now. We'll just feel a little pinch." She got the stent in with barely a nip. Pluralization or no, she was good. She snapped the gloves off. "All done. Doctors will be back in a minute. Do you want the info for the Getty? I don't think there will be space, but maybe someone cancelled?"

"Thanks, Fran. I'm good."

***

Doctor Solis knew better than to kill me with "we" and "our" or small talk. He wanted me in and out of there as much as I wanted to go, and the two other doctors in the room seemed equally sensitive to Solis's dominance.

"Any changes?" he asked, eyes on the monitor, fingers on keys as Doctor Nu slipped the thin tube through the stent. "Still off spicy food?"

"Hate it."

"Too bad. How's the wind been on your allergies?"

"I don't have allergies." I felt the tube slipping across my shoulder through a vein. It was truly uncomfortable. Not painful, but I had to think hard to keep from clawing through my skin to get the invading thing out.

"Chart says different." Dr. Solis checked Dr. Nu's work and looked at me. "You need to pay attention. Denial is your enemy. Your silly new allergies can turn into an infection you won't be able to fight. With the drought and the wind, my wife is eating Claritin like candy, even in the middle of February."

"Valentine's Day," I said more to myself than him.

"Any plans?" Dr. Solis asked, eyes on the tube, then the screen, then back.

"We're in," Dr. Nu called, one hand on the tube, and I felt it.

"Indeed," Solis said. "Breathe, Mister Drazen. Breathe."

***

How fast could I pull something together? Something huge. Something the size of my love, my respect, my devotion. It was our first Valentine's together, and Christmas had been such a disaster that I felt as if I needed to make it up to Monica tenfold. But when I got home from the biopsy, Lil had to help me to the door.

"Where's the missus today?" she asked. "Do you need me to get her?"

"Leave her alone. She's in the studio." Lil put me on the couch, and my body wanted to stay there forever.

"Mister Drazen, I don't want to pressure you, but I hope you didn't forget—"

"I forgot."

"I can pick up a dozen roses."

"Sure, Lil. Sure. Great idea."

She left to do the impossible: find a dozen roses on Valentine's Day for a man so enervated he couldn't do it himself.

"Fuck you," I whispered to heaven, my first sentiment of ingratitude in two months. "I'm getting over this."

My recovery was on track. I had no reason to be so angry, except that I was cheating Monica out of her entitlements, and her number one entitlement was me. From that couch to the stars above, I owed her myself.

I picked up the phone and called my friend Paul. We spoke briefly, then I closed my eyes for a few hours.

***

I woke with a buildup behind my face and a sneeze.

They say your heart skips a beat when you sneeze, so when I sneezed four more times, I panicked unreasonably. Then I panicked again when I realized the sun was setting and I was still on the couch.

"Fuck!"

On the table next to me were a dozen red roses, beautifully arranged, and an empty card and a pen. Thank God for Lil. I needed to give her more money.

I picked up my phone. Sneezed again. Multiple texts from Monica.

—Still here—

—Will be late—

—How did the biopsy go?—

*—Great session. Do you want
dinner with me for Valentine's?
Or are we skipping?—*

—Where are you?—

*—Please just tell me you're
ok or I'm leaving the studio
right now—*

The last one had come in minutes before and had probably gotten me to wake up. I tapped a fast response so she wouldn't panic. She panicked when I didn't respond, or when I breathed too hard, or slept too much or too little.

—Just got up—

*—thank you thank you thank
you—*

—Let me stretch and we'll talk
about tonight—

—No pressure but I hope
it involves your cock in my
mouth—

—But if not then ok I love
you—

I sneezed when I smiled. It was the fucking roses. Snot built up behind my face. My sinuses felt as if they would explode. According to my doctors, if the buildup settled in my sinuses or lungs, my suppressed immune system would allow an infection. And like everything else in the goddamn universe, it could kill me. So I threw out the roses.

***

I'd sent Lil to pick up Monica an hour earlier. It was Friday, so traffic from the west side would be brutal. From my vantage point at the Griffith Park Observatory, I could see the city in all its jam-packed glory. Streetlights held their grid, and the car lights along Wilshire crawled. She was there, somewhere, on her way to me.

I hoped I'd pulled this off as if I'd planned better. Paul, the director of the observatory, had taken me to a stone veranda inaccessible to the public and let in caterers to set up a dinner for two overlooking Los Angeles. I had candles, heat lamps, chafing dishes, everything I could manage for her. Below me, clusters of tourists shifted on well-worn paths, their laughter and voices drifting up to me without meaning. They'd be gone in an hour when the museum closed, and we'd be here, on our perch above the city.

I'd texted and called, letting Monica know Lil would pick her up, but I hadn't heard back. Once I told her I was fine, she probably shut the phone off to work. I considered the possibility that she was still in the studio, and would be until the wee hours of the morning, in which case I'd pack up dinner and go home, grateful she'd forgotten the holiday as well.

My phone rang.

"Hi, Lil. Where are you?"

"She's gone, sir. Sorry, I've been looking, but it turns out she left."

"Thanks. Head home. She probably went there."

I called my wife, confident I wasn't disturbing studio time. "Goddess?"

"Where are you?"

"I'm at a surprise location. Lil is—"

"You have to come home," she said, her voice raspy from a day of abusing it.

"No, you have to come here."

"Jonathan."

"Monica."

"I spent a week on this."

I argued a little more after that, but she'd spent time on whatever it was, whereas I'd thrown something together because a medical technician had reminded me of the date eight hours earlier. I had the staff pack up everything.

***

Lil had gotten to me quickly. She pulled up to the front but didn't go past the gate.

"Can you make it in from here?" she called back to me. "I'm not supposed to go past the gate."

"You knew?"

"Well, no. I just got a call. She thought you'd be napping, but then this whole thing happened instead. Sorry. At least you have the roses I picked up."

"Thank you, by the way."

"My pleasure."

I got out. The gate had a door-sized entry, and I went in that way. All the front lights were out, but Monica had put little paper lights along the drive, and I followed them to the house.

"The paper lights were going to go down the stairs," she said. "But they're fine outside too."

She was naked on my porch.

Our porch.

"I love what you're wearing," I said.

"My mom got it for me." She put her hands behind her back.

Had I thought she was too thin? She was perfect, her skin lit by candles and the moon, her hair falling over her shoulders like a scarf. I got on the step below her and touched her belly.

"You poor woman," I said, kissing the space between her breasts. Peaches and honey. Her scent. I rubbed her skin, releasing the smell, and put my tongue on her nipple and sucked. My hands went down her back until I reached her clasped fingers. I took hers in mine.

"I need you, Jonathan. I had a whole speech prepared. But I forgot it."

"I'm sorry you had to wait."

"Can you take me? Please."

"No pressure?"

She reached for my crotch, and I let her.

"Oh, you're hard."

"Very."

She pulled me to a chair and sat me down. She got on her knees. Nothing could have pleased me more than her, naked, on my porch, kneeling before me. I put my hands in her hair as she took out my dick. I didn't like her controlling the situation, but maybe it was the new heart that didn't find it too offensive. Maybe I'd changed in more ways than one.

Her mouth was eager, her throat open for an aria. Her hands stayed behind her back. I knew what I would have done before the surgery. I would have jammed her head onto me. I would have gone fast just to make it more difficult for her. I would have been hard and cruel and derived satisfaction from her discomfort. But not that day.

She looked up at me, letting my dick pop out of her mouth. "Is it okay?"

"Get up here," I said. "Straddle me. Let's give this a go."

"Really?"

"Don't make me say it twice."

She was up in a flash, thighs around me, eager hands around my base. "Fuck, Jonathan. You're so hard."

I put my hands on either side of her face and brought it to mine. "I own you," I whispered.

"I love you too." She hitched herself up, until the head of my dick was at her opening and her hands were on the back of the chair. "Are you ready?"

"Yes."

I put downward pressure on my hands, and gingerly and slowly, she lowered herself onto me. She was wet and tight, and when she pulled up, the sensation of being pleasurably sucked overwhelmed me. I groaned. She slid down then up again. We kissed, breathed on each other's faces, and kissed again.

I put my thumb on her clit, stroking up and down as she moved against me. In my life, I came when I wanted to and not a minute before. I listened for any number of physical signs so I knew when to hold back. One of them was my heart rate. So when the buildup in my groin happened without a feeling in my chest, I missed the opportunity to catch myself.

"I'm sorry," I moaned. "I'm coming."

"Come for me."

She moved faster. I wasn't in control. My body was betraying me. I had to give it up again. I came so hard I called her name to heaven.

Then I sneezed.

"Bless you."

"Tha—"

Sneeze.

"Bless—"

Sneeze.

"How many more you got?"

I shrugged behind my hand. *Sneeze.*

She got off me. "Let me get you a tissue."

She was up and through the front door before I could tell her I had a hankie. Then I knew what was causing the sneezing. I got up and stood in the doorway.

The living room was bedecked in roses.

She trotted down the stairs, still naked, carrying a box of tissues. "You were supposed to see this first. But I wasn't about to say no on the porch."

Sneeze.

She handed me the box.

"Monica, I'm—" *Sneeze.* I waved at a cluster of yellow roses. "Why the yellow?"

"There's a red rose for every day I've known you. A yellow for every day you were in the hospital. And one white." She swallowed hard, and her mouth screwed up to one side. "For the day I thought you died." Her eyes went wet.

I successfully held back a sneeze.

"I know what you think," she said. "I know you're worried about the recovery. And our sex life. You think you're hiding it and being all strong, but I see it. I wanted to let you know— well, before I seduced you—that it didn't matter. It takes what it takes. I'll wait forever for you. Every day, I'm glad you're alive."

"My goddess. I'm so sorry." I kissed her before she could protest, then I sneezed again. "We have to get rid of the roses, but first, I'm taking you upstairs. I'm fucking you as much as you deserve."

"You're dressed up." She stepped back and looked me up and down as if she was seeing me for the first time. "Where were you when you called?"

"Not telling. It's the idea for your birthday dinner now."

"I ruined your Valentine's dinner."

"I'm throwing your roses out."

"We suck at this."

I sneezed and took her upstairs to fuck her as much as she deserved. And she deserved everything.